Kane/Miller Book Publishers, Inc.
La Jolla, California

First published by Kane/Miller Book Publishers, Inc., 2008

All rights reserved. For information contact:
Kane/Miller Book Publishers, Inc.
P.O. Box 8515
La Jolla, CA 92038
www.kanemiller.com

Library of Congress Control Number: 2007932520
Printed and bound in China
1 2 3 4 5 6 7 8 9 10

ISBN: 978-1-933605-66-1

No! That's Wrong!

By Zhaohua Ji and Cui Xu

Kane/Miller
BOOK PUBLISHERS

It's a hat!

No, that's wrong. It's not a hat.

No, that's wrong. It's not a hat.

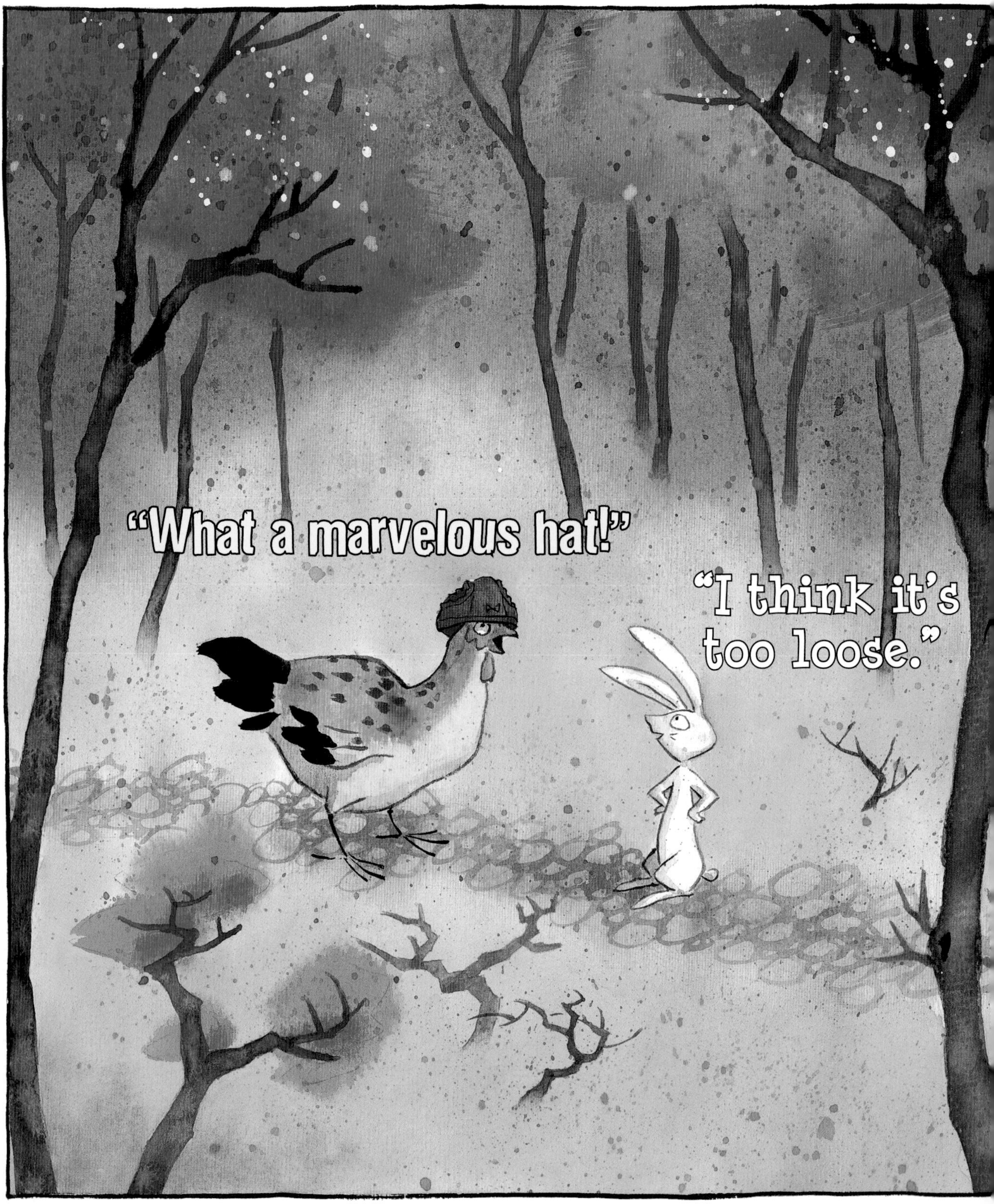
"What a marvelous hat!"
"I think it's too loose."

No, that's wrong. It's not a hat.

No, that's wrong. It's not a hat.

"What are you doing?
Why are you wearing
underpants on your head?"

"It's not a hat.
They're underpants."

"It's a hat."

Yes, that's right. They're underpants.

It's not a hat!"

That's right! It's not a hat.

That's right! That's how you wear underpants.

They're underpants.

Don't listen! They're underpants!

It's a wonderful hat!